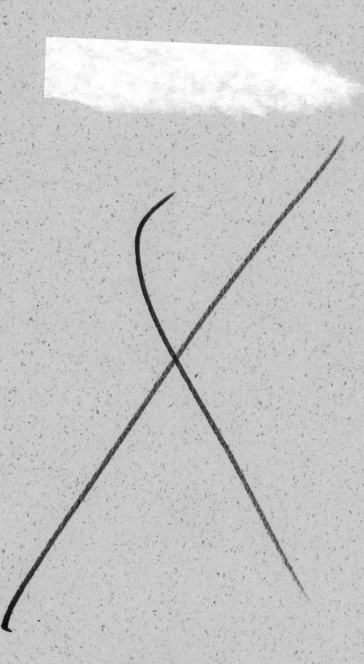

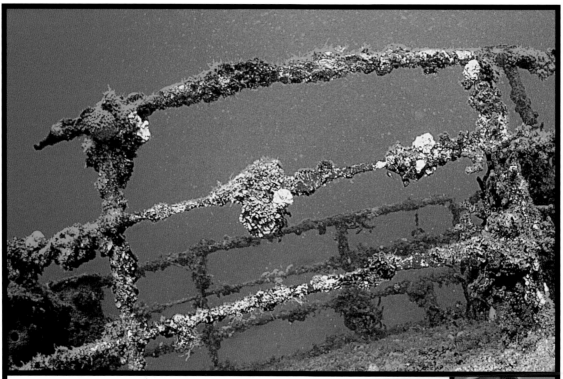

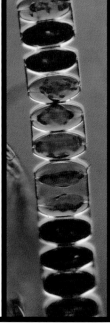

Published by Creative Education
123 South Broad Street, Mankato, Minnesota 56001
Creative Education is an imprint of The Creative Company

Design and production by Stephanie Blumenthal
Printed in the United States of America

Photographs by Tom Stack & Associates (Erwin & Peggy Bauer, Ken Davis, David Fleetham, Jeff Foott, Lynn Gerig,
Sharon Gerig, Joe McDonald, Randy Morse, Michael Nolan, Brian Parker, Milton Rand, Ed Robinson,
Mike Severns, Therisa & Tom Stack, Tsado / NASA, Tsado / NOAA, Greg Vaughn, David & Tess Young)

Library of Congress Cataloging-in-Publication Data

Bodden, Valerie.
Oceans / by Valerie Bodden.
p. cm. — (Our world)
Includes index.
ISBN-13 : 978-1-58341-464-4
1. Ocean—Juvenile literature. I. Title. II. Series.
GC21.5.B65 2006   551.46—dc22   2005053718

First Edition
2 4 6 8 9 7 5 3 1

OUR WORLD

O
C
E
A
N
S

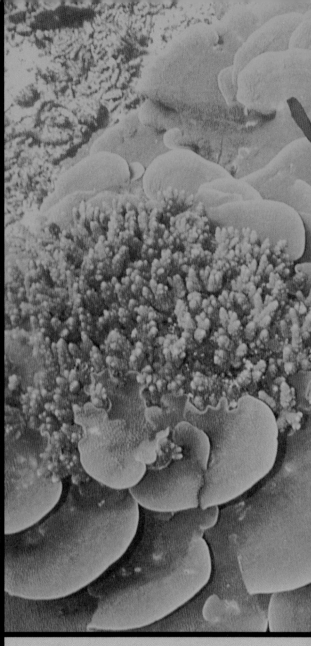

Valerie Bodden

Oceans are big **bodies** of water. They are found all over Earth. The biggest ocean in the world is called the Pacific Ocean.

The water in oceans has salt in it. It is called salt-water. In some places, oceans are deep. The water is way over your head! In other places, oceans are **shallow**. You can stand in the water. Some oceans are warm. Other oceans are cold.

Oceans are pretty above and below the water

The water in oceans moves in waves. The waves go up and down. When it storms, some waves get very big. They can be taller than a house!

*Some waves are gentle;
other waves are powerful*

There are **islands** in some oceans. Some

islands are full of trees and flowers. Others are sandy.

Some are rocky. People live on some islands. Lots of animals live on other islands.

Islands rise up out of the water

Lots of birds live near oceans. Seagulls are birds. They live near oceans. Penguins are birds, too. They swim in some oceans.

There are lots of seagulls by oceans

Lots of plants live in oceans. Seaweed is a plant. It grows on the bottom of oceans. Seaweed can be short or tall. Most seaweed is green. But some is brown or red.

Some seaweed has big, flat leaves

Lots of fish swim in oceans. The fish come in many colors. Some fish are yellow. Others are blue. Some are orange. Others are green. Some fish are lots of colors! Some fish are tiny. Others are huge!

Some fish swim in big groups called schools

*Many different
animals
live in oceans*

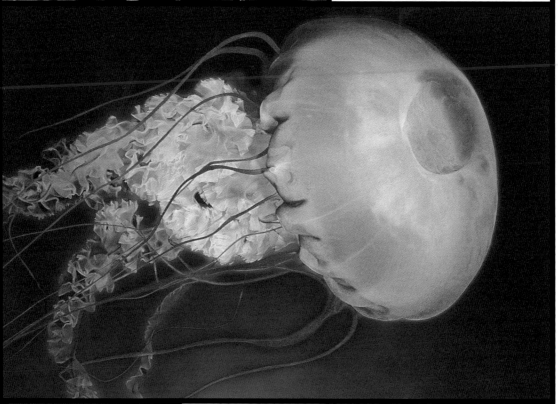

Other animals live in oceans, too. Dolphins swim in oceans. So do **jellyfish**. Shrimp and starfish live in oceans. **Eels** live there, too.

Lots of people like to visit oceans. Some people sit on the beach. Some pick up seashells. Others swim. Some people dive deep under the water. Some ride in boats. Others go fishing. There are lots of ways to have fun at the ocean!

People wear special clothes to dive in oceans

Waves can be fun to watch. You can see them move up and down. Next time you go to a lake or the ocean, find a flat piece of wood. Throw it into the water. Watch it move. Does it get closer to you? Or does it just move up and down? What happens to a ball thrown into the water?

GLOSSARY

bodies—areas filled with lots of water

eels—ocean animals that look like snakes

islands—small areas of land with water all around them

jellyfish—ocean animals that are round and almost clear

shallow—not deep

LEARN MORE ABOUT OCEANS

Monterey Bay Aquarium:
Coloring Pages
http://www.mbayaq.org/lc/
activities/coloring_pages.asp

Ocean Animals Activities for Kids
http://www.dltk-kids.com/
animals/ocean.html

Oceans for Youth: Kids' Corner
http://www.oceansforyouth.
com/kidscorner.html

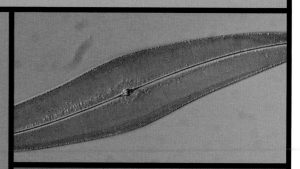